Bamboo for *Me*, Bamboo for *You!*

This book is for you,
Karen Krugman and James Woo! —F. M.

For my mother, for everything —P. H.

ALADDIN

An imprint of Simon & Schuster Children's Publishing Division

1230 Avenue of the Americas, New York, New York 10020

First Aladdin hardcover edition November 2017

Text copyright © 2017 by Fran Manushkin

Illustrations copyright © 2017 by Purificación Hernández

All rights reserved, including the right of reproduction in whole or in part in any form.

ALADDIN and related logo are registered trademarks of Simon & Schuster, Inc.

For information about special discounts for bulk purchases, please contact

Simon & Schuster Special Sales at 1-866-506-1949 or business@simonandschuster.com.

The Simon & Schuster Speakers Bureau can bring authors to your live event.

For more information or to book an event contact the Simon & Schuster Speakers Bureau

at 1-866-248-3049 or visit our website at www.simonspeakers.com.

Book designed by Karin Paprocki

The illustrations for this book were rendered digitally.

The text of this book was set in Oneleigh Pro Bold & Italic.

Manufactured in China 0817 SCP

2 4 6 8 10 9 7 5 3 1

Library of Congress Control Number 2016962807

ISBN 978-1-4814-5063-8 (hc)

ISBN 978-1-4814-5064-5 (eBook)

Bamboo for *Me,* Bamboo for *You!*

By Fran Manushkin

Illustrated by Purificación Hernández

ALADDIN

New York London Toronto Sydney New Delhi

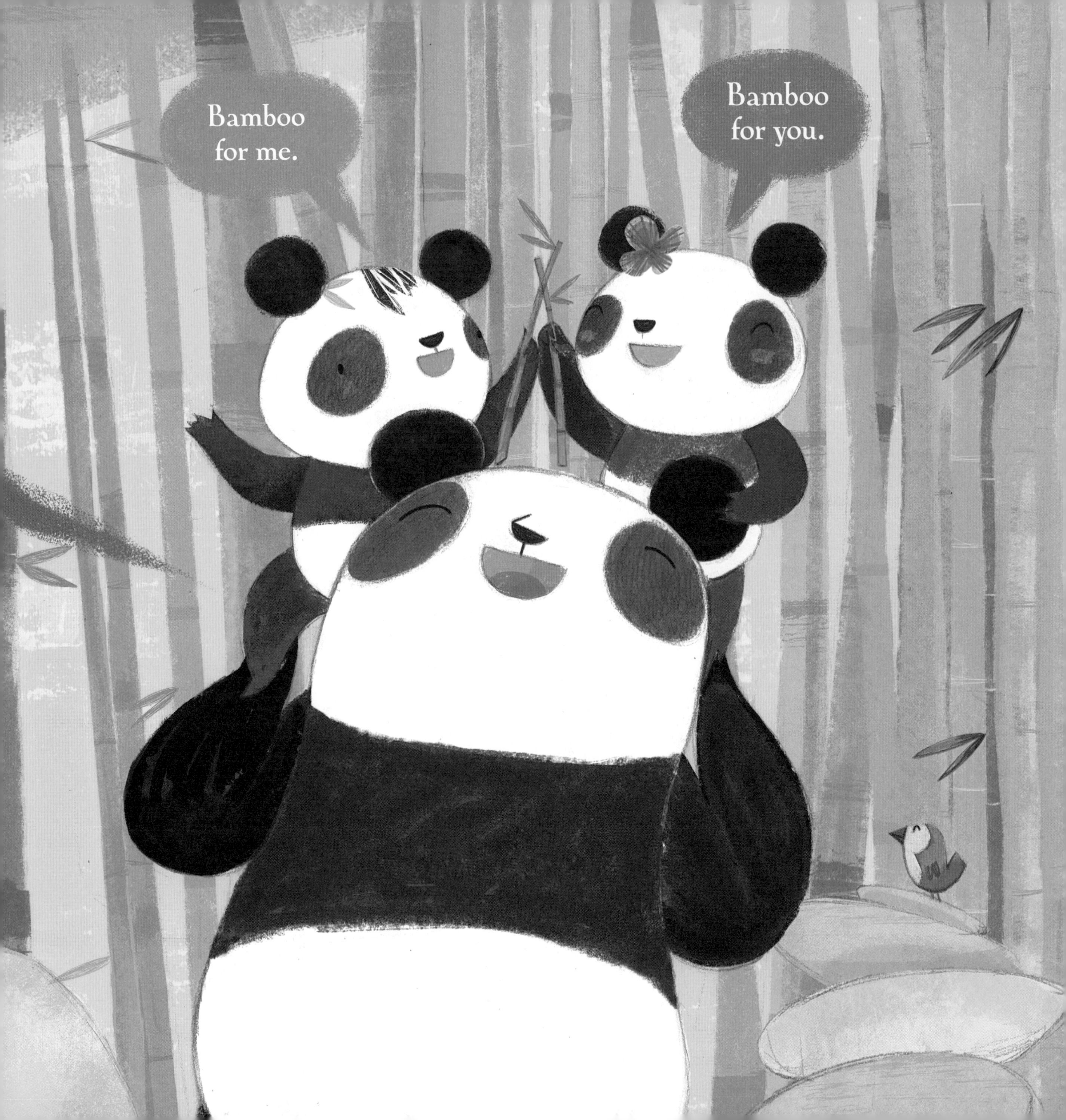
Bamboo
for me.
Bamboo
for you.

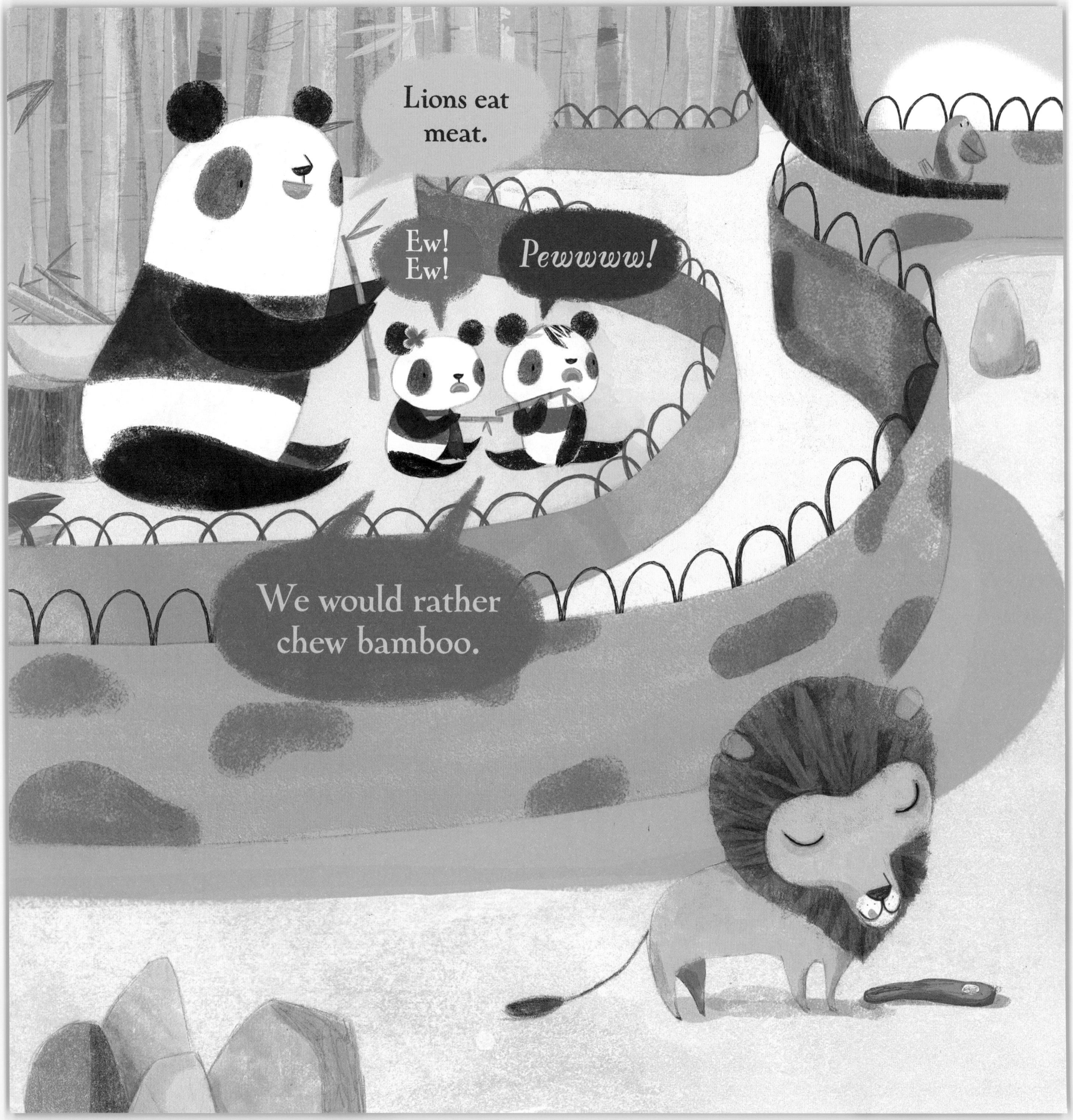
Lions eat meat.
Ew! Ew!
Pewwww!
We would rather chew bamboo.

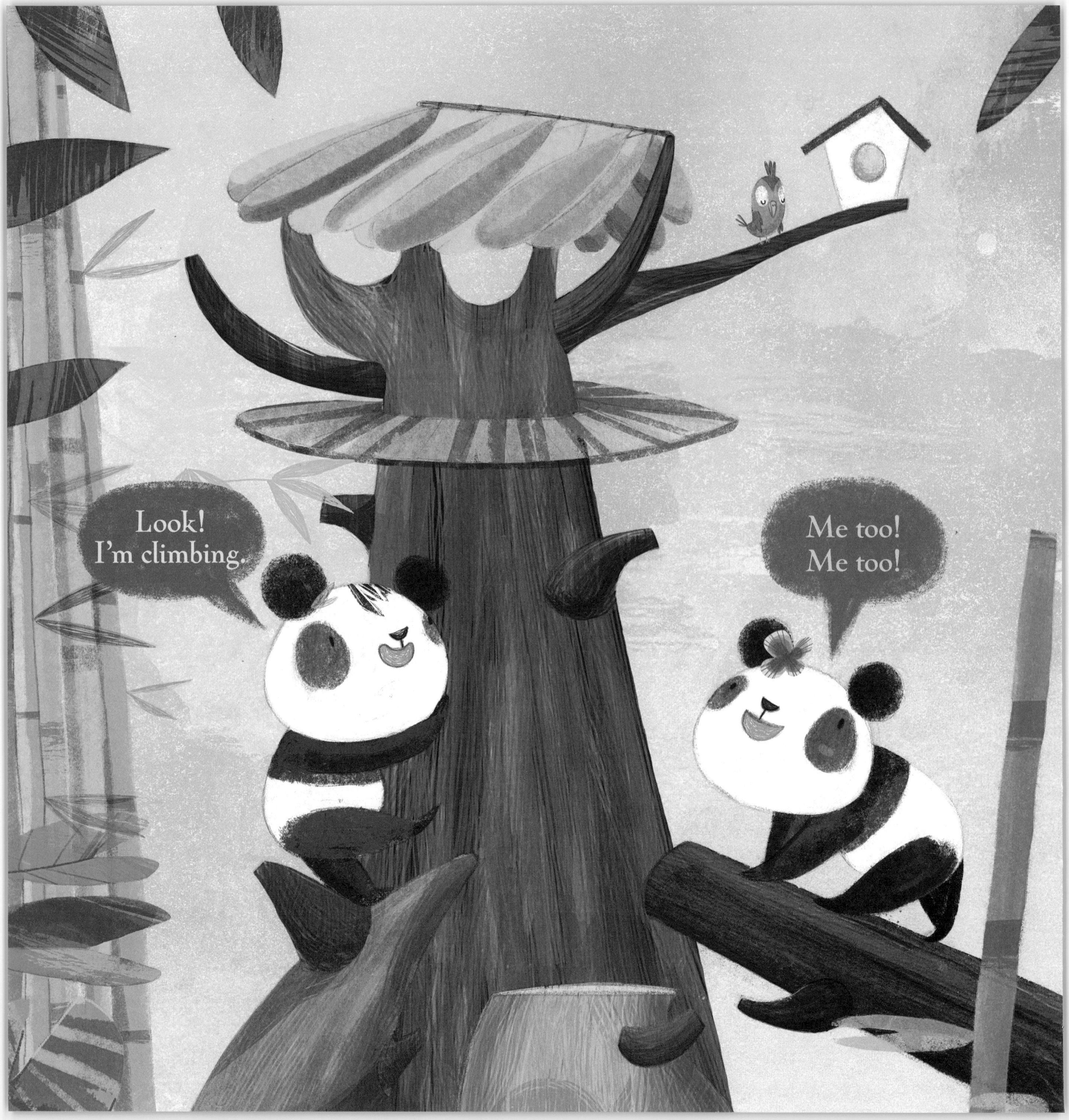
Look!
I’m climbing.
Me too!
Me too!

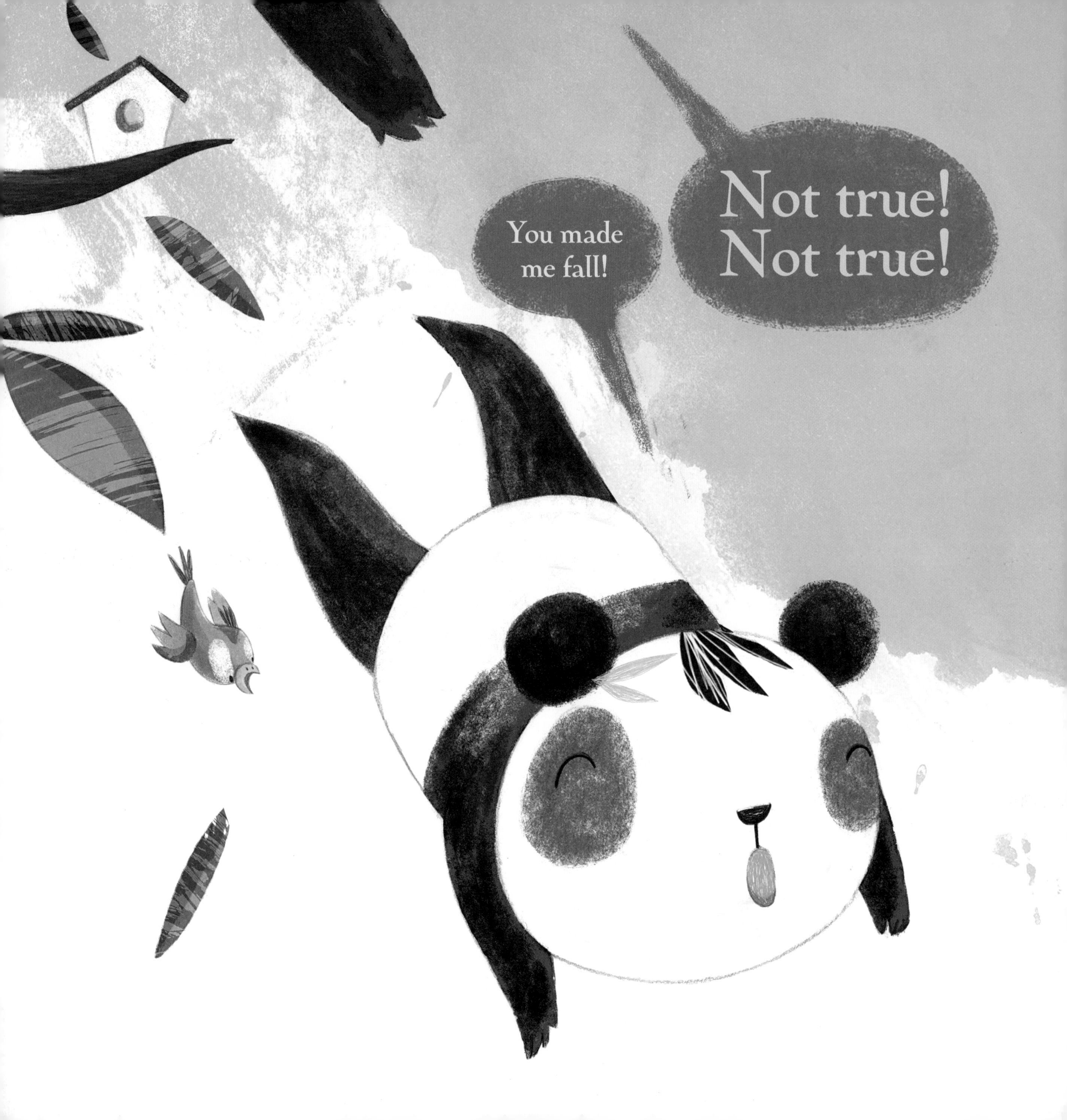
You made me fall!
Not true! Not true!

It's *hard* to hide behind bamboo.

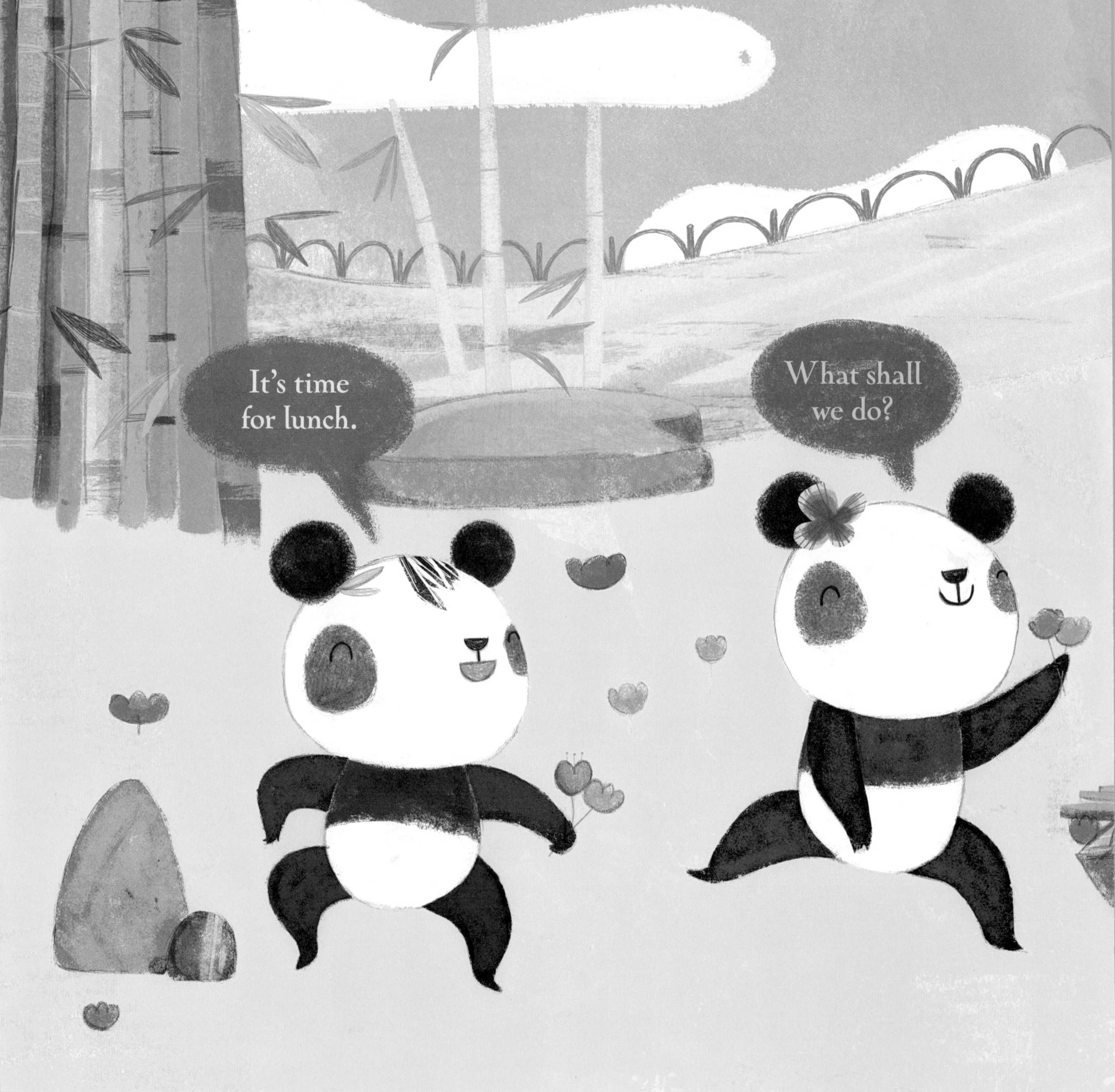
It's time for lunch.
What shall we do?

I don't
like to
fight with
you.

Dear cubs, there's room for both of you.

Sleep tight,
Amanda.

You sleep tight too,
with dreams of lots
of sweet . . .

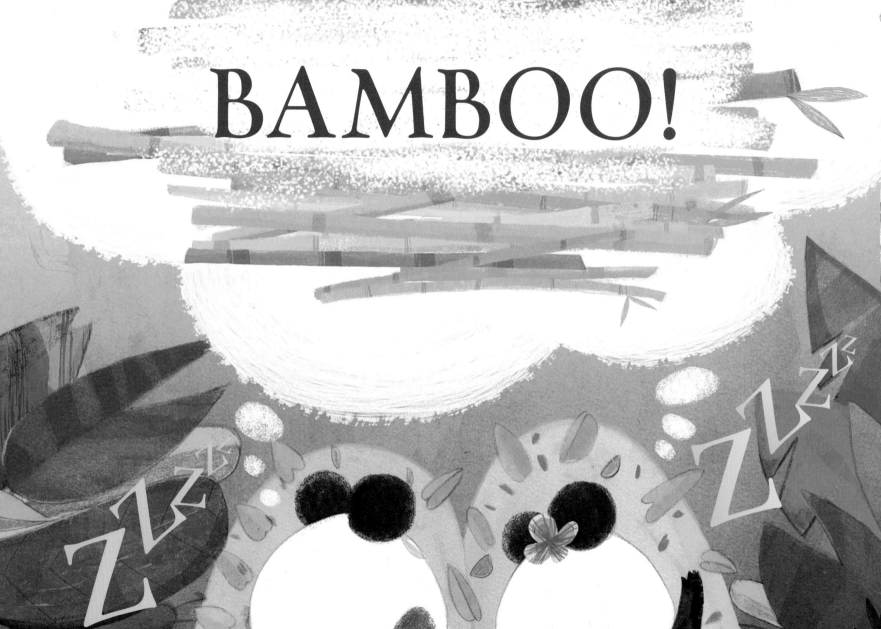